SHONEN JUMP'S

Yu-Gi-Oh! GX

Back to Duel

Adapted by Tracey West

SCHOLASTIC INC.
New York Toronto London Auckland Sydney
Mexico City New Delhi Hong Kong Buenos Aires

No part of this publication may be reproduced, stored in a retrieval system, or transmitted in any form or by any means, electronic, mechanical, photocopying, recording, or otherwise, without written permission of the publisher. For information regarding permission, write to Scholastic Inc., Attention: Permissions Department, 557 Broadway, New York, NY 10012.

ISBN-13: 978-0-439-88835-6
ISBN-10: 0-439-88835-2

© 2007 Kazuki Takahashi • NAS•TV TOKYO
© 1996 Kazuki Takahashi
© 2004 NAS•TV TOKYO

Published by Scholastic Inc.
SCHOLASTIC and associated logos are trademarks and/or registered trademarks of Scholastic Inc.

12 11 10 9 8 7 6 5 4 3 2 1   7 8 9 10 11 12/0

Printed in the U.S.A.
First printing, October 2007

◆ CHAPTER ONE ◆

CHANCELLOR CROWLER?

If you want to be a Duel Master, everyone knows the best place to go: Duel Academy.

Students come from all over the world to learn the secrets of dueling. They compete for places in three dorms. The cream of the crop get to live in the fancy Obelisk Blue dorm. Rising stars get to live in the comfortable Ra Yellow dorm. Everyone else ends up in Slifer Red, a shady shack overlooking the sea.

A lot had happened at Duel Academy in the last year. An evil force threatened the school — and the world. But now a new school year was beginning.

As the morning sun dawned on the new day, two men ran toward the water. One man was tall and skinny.

He wore his blond hair in a ponytail. His long nose curved down toward his even longer chin. He wore black pants and a fancy blue jacket. Frilly white cuffs peeked out from under his sleeves.

The other man was small and very round. His thin mustache rested against his puffy cheeks. His brown hair curled up on either side of his head like two waves. He wore a fancy green uniform.

"Keep up, you Swedish meatball!" snapped the tall man, Vellian Crowler. "They're almost here!"

Bonaparte, the short man, huffed and puffed to keep up. "I'm French, you imbecile!" he shot back. "*Pardonne-moi* for not having longer legs! Besides, what's the rush about?"

"I *told* you, the freshmen," Crowler said. "Their boat is arriving as we speak!"

"So big whoop," Bonaparte replied. "Just because you've been promoted to school chancellor, all of a sudden you care? Surely you didn't drag me out here just to greet the new students? So fess up, monsieur."

They neared the shore of Academy Island, and Crowler stopped. He took a book of Duel Monsters stars out of his jacket and opened it up. He held out the book.

"Feast your eyes on *this*!" he told Bonaparte.

The open page showed a picture of a young man with big, blue eyes and silvery gray hair.

Bonaparte shrugged. "Did I miss the joke?" he asked.

"Are you calling Aster Phoenix a joke?" Crowler asked. Bonaparte gasped at the name. "Not only is this superstar the top-ranked duelist in the entire world, he's joined the freshman class of our very school!"

"There must be a mistake," Bonaparte said. "I mean, a world class professional going back to school? But why?"

"I don't know," Crowler shrugged. "But with a celebrity under my tutelage, I'll be famous! After all, everyone knows Aster Phoenix."

Crowler was right about that . . . almost.

Jaden Yuki stood on the shore of Academy Island, his brown eyes shining. His first year at Duel Academy had been unbelievable. He had battled evil duelists called Shadow Riders in mind-bending duels. He had put up with Professor Crowler, who didn't even want Jaden at the school. Jaden had helped save the school — and the world — from total destruction.

Now his second year of school was about to begin, and he was still stuck in the Slifer Red dorm.

That didn't bother Jaden one bit. He didn't mind being called a Slifer Slacker. As long as he got to duel, people could call him whatever they wanted.

He was about to begin a duel now. Jaden nodded at his opponent.

"Hey, kid!" he cried out. "I don't know who you are, but let's duel!"

Then Jaden stopped. "Whoops! Wrong catch phrase. What I meant to say was . . . get your game on!"

Jaden's best friend, Syrus Truesdale, watched the duel from a ridge overlooking the shore. Dorothy, the owner of the school's card shop, watched, too. She stroked a pale brown cat that sat on her lap.

"Day one and Jaden's already dueling," Dorothy said. "But with who?"

"Beats me," Syrus replied. "But he definitely looks familiar."

"So what's your name, freshman?" Jaden called out.

Jaden's opponent smiled. He was a tall boy with big,

blue eyes and silvery gray hair. He wore a neat white suit and a gray tie.

"You can call me A.P.," he answered.

Jaden didn't get it. He was facing Aster Phoenix, the top duelist in the world, and he had no clue.

"All right," Jaden said. "Let's throw down, *Ap*!"

• CHAPTER TWO •

STRANGE MOVES

"You ready, freshman?" Jaden asked.

Aster smiled. "Bring it!"

Up on the ridge, two more people arrived to watch the duel. Alexis was a tall, pretty girl with long, light brown hair. She wore the blue and white uniform of the Obelisk dorm.

Chazz had spiky black hair and gray eyes. A couple of years ago, he would have been wearing the Obelisk Blue uniform, too. But Chazz had left Duel Academy for a while, and when he came back, he ended up in a spare room in the Slifer Red dorm. He didn't consider himself a Slifer, though, and he wore a black uniform instead of a red one.

"Wow, Jaden doesn't waste any time, does he?" Alexis remarked.

"It figures he challenged a freshman," Chazz sneered.

Syrus shook his head. "Actually, that guy challenged *him*," he explained. "He just showed up at our dorm and was all, 'I'm here to throw down with the best duelist in the Academy. And from what I hear, that's Jaden Yuki.'"

Syrus looked down at Jaden and Aster. The morning sun reflected off of Syrus's glasses. "That brings us here," he went on. "Take a closer look. I could swear I've seen that guy before."

Jaden activated his Duel Disk. Aster did the same. The two boys faced each other. A long stretch of rocky sand separated them.

Alexis studied Aster for a moment. "You're right!" she told Syrus.

"Yeah, he does look familiar," Chazz agreed.

Pharaoh, the brown cat, purred in Dorothy's plump lap. The cat used to belong to Professor Banner, the former head of the Slifer Red dorm. After a series of strange events, Banner's soul was now housed inside the cat. Now, Dorothy takes care of Pharaoh.

"Hey, Chazz," Dorothy said. "Maybe he graduated from that snooty prep school of yours."

"Good call!" Syrus agreed. He eyed Aster's expensive-looking suit. "He definitely looks rich *and* stuck-up enough."

Chazz scowled. "Look, shrimp. He's nothing like me!"

Down below, Aster held up his first card. "Ojama Yellow in Defense Mode!"

Chazz gasped as a tiny yellow Duel Monster appeared in front of Aster. Using Ojama cards was *Chazz's* specialty!

"Ojama? Are you sure?" Jaden asked. Ojama Yellow did have 1000 defense points, but other than that it wasn't considered to be a very powerful card. You needed strategy to make Ojama cards work — and using an Ojama Yellow card on the very first turn was definitely *not* good strategy.

Chazz recovered from his surprise. "Told you we're not alike," he told Syrus. "That's gotta be one of the dumbest moves I've ever seen. I would never start out with a lame card like that!"

The spirit of Chazz's Ojama Yellow card appeared on his shoulder. The little monster's round eyes danced on the end of two long eyestalks. The only clothing it wore on its chubby body was a skimpy red bathing suit bottom.

"You'd save the best for last, right boss? Right?" Ojama Yellow asked.

"Wrong," Chazz snapped. "Now beat it, pit stain!"

"I love it when you use my pet name!" Ojama Yellow said. Then it vanished.

"Excuse me?" Alexis asked. She couldn't see or hear Ojama Yellow.

"Oh, nothing," Chazz said quickly.

"Whatever," Alexis replied. She looked down thoughtfully at Aster. "I wonder what *else* he has in his deck?"

"Not much, I bet," Dorothy said.

"Wait, how do you know that?" Syrus asked.

"It's simple," Dorothy explained. "He just assembled that deck this morning from random cards in the campus card shop. He was very confident. He said he could win a duel with pretty much anything. I told him he wouldn't last long at the school by building a deck with random cards. But he said it was just a temporary deck, for some kind of test."

Chazz shook his head. Any good duelist knew you

had to carefully build your deck. You had to know your cards better than your own friends if you wanted to win.

"Give me a break," Chazz said. "Who duels with left-over cards?"

"*That* guy," Alexis pointed out.

Jaden was anxious to make his move.

"Here goes!" he called out. "Looks like class is in session! So meet your teacher — Elemental Hero Sparkman!"

Jaden held up the card, and a hero monster in a blue and gold uniform flashed next to him — along with 1600 attack points.

"Okay, freshman. I think it's time for your first Duel Academy lesson!" Jaden cried.

Sparkman charged across the dueling field. Streaks of white lightning flashed around his body. Jagged bolts of electricity shot from the palms of his hands.

Wham! The blast destroyed Ojama Yellow. The monster vanished from the field.

Aster watched the action with a calm smile on his face.

"Some things you gotta learn the hard way, right?" Jaden said. "But trust me, *I* can teach you way more than some lame school lecture."

"Wow, so I guess it's true," Aster said. "You *are* as good as they say."

"Thanks for the props," Jaden said, grinning. "But when you play cards like Ojama you don't exactly make it too tough. What did you do, take lessons from Chazz or something?"

"Hey!" Chazz protested.

Aster fanned out the cards in his hand. "Let's do this again, shall we?" he said.

Soon I'll learn all of Jaden's strategies, Aster thought to himself. *All I have to do is play weak cards.*

Aster looked back up at Jaden. "I'll play this face-down, and — "

Suddenly, a loud beeping sound filled the air.

"What's the deal?" Jaden asked, frowning.

"It's cool," Aster said, reaching for his back pocket. "Just my cell phone."

Jaden was shocked. Aster answered the call.

"It's me," he said cheerfully. "What's up?"

"Who whips out a cell phone in the middle of a duel?" Chazz asked. "That's obnoxious."

"Yeah, no joke," Syrus agreed. "He really *is* like you, Chazz."

Aster kept talking, and now Jaden was furious. This freshman was way rude!

"Calm down," he told himself. "He's a freshman. You were a crazy kid like him last year, Jaden."

Aster smiled and kept talking. "That's right," he said. "I'm dueling him as we speak."

But the man on the other end of the phone was not your average friendly phone caller. He wore a white robe with a hood that covered his face. He sat at a table with fortune-telling cards arranged in a pattern in front of him, face down. He turned over one of the cards.

"Excellent," he told Aster.

"So any last minute words of advice?" Aster asked.

The mysterious man turned over a card. "The reaper of souls is in reverse," he said. "You know what must be done."

"Absolutely!" Aster answered. "Thanks for the call!"

Jaden had no idea who Aster was talking to, and he didn't care.

"All right!" he cried. "Get your phone *off* and your game *on*!"

• CHAPTER THREE •

SANCTUARY IN THE SKY

"So you're actually gonna play a good card this time, right?" Jaden asked Aster.

Aster smiled innocently. "Oh, you mean something like this one," he said. He held up a card from his hand. "It's a spell card called Reload! And here's how it works. First, I toss all my cards. Then I put them right back in my deck and redraw!"

Jaden watched in amazement as Aster put all of the cards in his hand back in his deck.

"Wait. So you're getting a do-over?" he asked.

"You said yourself I needed better cards," Aster said, shuffling his deck. "So I thought I'd start over."

"I knew that," Jaden said, covering up his surprise. "Way to follow my advice, freshman!"

Then Jaden sighed. "Being a mentor is hard work. So tell me. What else have you learned from dueling an upperclassman like me?"

Aster looked at the new cards in his hand and grinned. He put one of the cards in his Duel Disk.

"This!" Aster answered. "I activate The Sanctuary in the Sky!"

A huge tunnel of light appeared between the duelists, and Jaden knew that Aster had played a field card. A big, gold building rose up behind Aster. A staircase made of gold bricks led to a majestic-looking building held up by thick columns. A golden orb on a tall staff topped the building. Fluffy clouds floated around the sanctuary.

"So you played a big building on some clouds," Jaden said, teasing his opponent. "Exactly what *I* would have done. Glad I could help!"

Aster smiled. "So then I guess you knew I'd play

this!" he cried, holding up another card. "Warrior of Zera!"

A muscled warrior in green armor appeared — and then vanished just as quickly.

"But here's a little twist for you," Aster continued. "I'm sacrificing it to summon Archlord Zerato!"

A bigger, tougher-looking warrior appeared in place of Warrior Zera. Archlord Zerato had huge wings and wore a green helmet with red horns on top. The massive warrior had an impressive 2800 attack points.

"And here's a little something else you might not have expected," Aster went on. "I'm sending my Mystical Shine Ball to the graveyard, and it takes all of your monsters with it!"

Aster put the card in his graveyard. The golden orb on top of Sanctuary in the Sky began to glow. A glowing light shone from the ball, zapping Jaden's Sparkman. The monster disappeared.

"And now, Archlord Zerato, strike his life points directly!" Aster cried.

Archlord Zerato flew into the air, and Jaden shielded himself. Zerato pummeled Jaden with a shower of glowing projectiles. Jaden's life points dropped from 4000 all the way to 1200.

"Wow, that's serious," Syrus remarked on the sideline. "It's like this one time, at duel camp, when an Archlord attacked me, and — "

"Zip it, twerp," Chazz said.

Aster looked across the field. The attack had brought Jaden to his knees.

"That's all for now," Aster said. "Hey, you okay?"

Jaden stood up, smiling. "Okay? You kidding? I've been waiting all summer for a match like this! And the best part is, it's my move!"

Jaden pulled a card from his hand. "I summon Elemental Hero Clayman in defense mode!"

The big, bulky hero appeared in front of Jaden, with a hefty 2000 defense points.

"And next, I activate my Metamorphosis spell card!" Jaden said. "Then I sacrifice Clayman to summon Elemental Hero Clay Guardian!"

Clay Guardian appeared in Clayman's position. He had massive stone arms, and a round, rocklike head. A huge red shield protected his body.

"Patrol Penalty!" Jaden yelled.

"What's that?" Aster asked. But before Jaden could answer, Aster saw his life points begin to drop. "Tell me!"

"I'd be glad to," Jaden said. "You see, you just lost six hundred points. Two hundred for each of your cards."

Aster frowned as his life points dropped to 3400.

"Now I'll throw down a facedown," Jaden said, putting the card face down on his Duel Disk. "And then I think I'll call it quits."

It was Aster's turn now, but Jaden wasn't worried.

"Now let me lay it down for you," Jaden told him. "Your first problem is that you managed to use up every card in your hand."

Jaden continued his lecture, acting like a Duel Academy professor.

"Exhibit B," Jaden went on, "your Archlord has the same number of points my Clay Guardian has. So your chance of winning is like, only ninety-five percent!"

"Excuse me, oh wise one, but aren't those good odds?" Aster asked.

Jaden laughed to cover up his embarrassment. "I was just testing you."

Up on the ridge, Alexis shook her head.

"Real smooth," she said.

"How did Jaden make it past the review board?" Chazz wondered.

"Wait, so you mean his math was wrong?" Syrus asked.

Down on the field, Aster drew more cards.

"All I need now is a monster that's stronger than yours," Aster said. "So let's see what fate has in store for me."

"It's not about fate," Jaden replied. "It's about listening. Take me. I'm always listening to what my cards have to say."

"You really are nuts," Aster said in disbelief. "You expect me to have a conversation with my cards?"

"Yeah, try using your cell phone," Jaden joked. "Maybe send a text message. Hey, they just might answer!"

Just then, the spirit of Winged Kuriboh floated next to Jaden's head. Jaden had a special relationship with the card. But only he could see Winged Kuriboh. He winked at his friend.

Aster studied Jaden. "This kid isn't what I expected at all," Aster muttered to himself. "I mean, he gives useless advice, he can't compute a simple math problem, and to top it all off he hears voices in his head. I guess it's time to end this duel and move on with my life!"

*   *   *

Aster's mysterious friend in the white hood tracked the progress of the duel. But he didn't use a video camera or computer. He used his fortune-telling cards.

He turned over another card facing him.

"Ah, the Inverted Chariot," he said. "A forewarning that the end is near!"

◄ • CHAPTER FOUR • ►

ELEMENTAL HERO TEMPEST!

"Remember, freshman, listen to your deck!" Jaden called to Aster.

"Whatever," Aster said flatly. He pulled a new card from his hand. Then he made a face and sighed loudly.

"Bad card, huh?" Jaden asked. "You might want to work on that poker face a bit."

"Perhaps," Aster said. "Or maybe I just want you to think it's a bad card. Or it could be that I don't want to win!"

Jaden couldn't believe what he was hearing. "And you called *me* nuts?"

"When you accepted my challenge, did you ever stop and ask yourself, what do I want? Why did I come here? And most importantly, out of everyone here, why did I challenge you?" Aster asked him. "Well, the truth is, I heard you were the best and I came here to test you."

"Come on, you can't be serious," Jaden replied. "Hel-lo! This is Duel Academy, bro. They give us tests in this place every day. But they're never as sweet as this!"

Aster gave a superior smile. "Of course they're not. Cause this duel's not about grades. It's about destiny!"

"What?" Jaden asked.

"Maybe my Beckoning Light will clear things up!" Aster announced. He held up a card. "Once I toss out my hand, a Light Attribute monster returns from my graveyard!"

Aster got rid of his cards. Then he took Mystical Shine Ball out from the graveyard.

"Then I'll use Zerato's effect again, and you know what that means, don't you?" Aster teased. "Your Guardian's a goner!"

Aster returned Mystical Shine Ball to the graveyard.

The orb on top of Sanctuary in the Sky glowed once again. It zapped Elemental Hero Clay Guardian. The massive hero vanished from the field. Now Jaden had no defense.

"See ya!" Aster said gleefully.

"Whoa, not bad!" Jaden admitted.

"You think that's impressive?" Aster asked. "Watch this. Archlord, attack him directly! Sacred Surge!"

Archlord Zerato rose into the air, ready to begin his attack. Jaden's friends gasped. Aster could win the duel with this move!

But Jaden was not ready to go down yet.

"Your Archlord's going to have to chill for a sec," Jaden said. "Cause I play Flute of Summoning Kuriboh! Which, if you couldn't tell, summons a Kuriboh!"

Jaden played his Winged Kuriboh. The furry creature appeared on the field with only 200 defense points. But that's all it needed to take the heat off of Jaden.

Archlord Zerato had no choice. It swooped down on Kuriboh, quickly defeating the little monster.

"Thanks for taking the hit, pal," Jaden told his friend. Then he grinned at Aster. "Now, what was all that business back there about destiny?"

"It's simple," Aster replied. "Everything that happens to us is planned out the day we're born. Losers are born to be losers, and legends are born to be legends."

"Legend? Who, me?" Jaden said. "Aw, come on. Hero, perhaps. Or maybe teen idol."

Alexis shook her head. "Someone stop him," she said.

"Well, at least he's having fun," Syrus pointed out.

"Glad someone is," Chazz muttered.

Jaden continued bragging. "I'm a superstar. Who knew? Well, I guess *I* did. Ha!"

Aster watched Jaden from across the field. He hadn't been sure what to expect when he faced Jaden in a duel. But he had never imagined this. . . .

Aster's mind flashed back to a meeting with the man in the white robe — his manager, Sartorius.

"Once you locate this Jaden Yuki, he is to defeat you, is that understood?" Sartorius had told him. "It is the only way I can be certain that he is indeed the One."

Aster hadn't liked that idea at all. "There's got to be another way," he said. "I've *never* thrown a duel!"

"Aster, have I ever once steered you wrong?" Sartorius said. "You must trust in me."

Aster frowned at the memory. *How can a manager tell his star player to lose?* he wondered.

Across the field, Jaden was ready to get back to action. "All right, it's the Legend's turn!" he called out. "So stand back!"

Jaden drew a card. "Sweet!" he cried. Then he slapped it down on his Duel Disk. "I play Elemental Hero Bubbleman!"

A big hero with a round face, blue costume, and white cape appeared. Bubbleman had 800 attack points.

"Now, if my field's empty, which it just so happens to be, then I get to draw two new cards from my deck," Jaden announced. He drew the two cards and studied them. "I'll throw a facedown, and then play this!"

Jaden held up a card. "The Warrior Returning Alive! Which means that one of my Warriors, well . . . returns . . . you know . . . alive."

Sparkman flashed onto the field.

Jaden chose another card. "And now I play Polymerization," he said. "How about that?"

Aster had nothing to say. Deep down, he had a hunch about what was coming.

"Oh, so the Legend has rendered you speechless, eh?" Jaden taunted Aster. "Well, this ought to get a reaction. I fuse Bubbleman, Avian, and Sparkman. . . ."

Elemental Hero Avian, a hero with big, white wings, appeared on the field next to Bubbleman and Sparkman. Then all three heroes vanished in a swirl of light.

". . . in order to create Elemental Hero Tempest!" Jaden cried.

Tempest had blue armor and a blue mask over his eyes. The feathers in his white wings looked like long, sharp swords. A metal weapon extended from his right arm.

"Put him away with Glider Strike!" Jaden told his hero.

Tempest flew up into the air, pointing a weapon at Archlord Zerato. The force of the attack shattered the Archlord.

"He'll lose!" Syrus moaned from the sidelines. He thought Tempest would be sent to the graveyard with Zerato's special ability.

But Jaden had another idea. He grinned at Aster.

"I'm sure you know that all I have to do is send one of my field cards to the graveyard. That way my Tempest can't be destroyed!"

Jaden's facedown card shattered. Now Tempest was safe.

"Now for the encore," Jaden said. "Check this out — De-Fusion! It transforms my Tempest back into Sparkman, Avian, and Bubbleman."

The three heroes appeared on the field once again.

"Bubbleman, you're up first!" Jaden cried.

Bubbleman blasted Aster directly with a powerful stream of water. Aster's life points dropped by 800.

"Avian, Quill Cascade!" Jaden yelled.

Avian's sharp feathers zipped across the field, attacking Aster. Now Aster's life points dropped down to 1600.

"Now, Sparkman, finish him off with Static Shockwave!" Jaden called out.

Sparkman pelted Aster with sizzling lightning bolts. Aster fell to his knees as his life points dropped down to zero.

Jaden pumped his fist in the air. "And that's game!"

• CHAPTER FIVE •

THE GAME IS STILL ON

"Hope my triple threat didn't rock you too hard," Jaden told Aster. He walked up to Aster to see if he was all right.

Aster rose to his feet. "Nah, I'm fine," he replied. "Nice game."

"Not bad," Jaden said. "For a freshman, that is."

"Gee, thanks," Aster said.

"You just keep on practicing, kid. Maybe you'll even be a legend some day. You know, like me!" Jaden laughed. "But that's a long way off. First you have to stop being so cocky. I mean, I'm great, but you don't see me bragging."

Dorothy watched Jaden and Aster talking down below. "What a duel, huh guys?" she asked Chazz, Syrus, and Alexis. "And that new mystery duelist is quite the looker, don't ya think? Did anyone catch his name?"

"Uh, A.P.?" Syrus guessed.

"So I guess I'll see you around, Ap!" Jaden told Aster.

Aster walked away from Jaden. He felt more confused than before. *I don't get it,* he thought. *Sure this Jaden kid is a decent duelist. But I don't see why my manager's so obsessed with him. And I still don't understand how joining this school helps my career . . .*

Aster climbed up the ridge and found himself facing Jaden's friends. Dorothy waved at him.

"Don't be a stranger, stranger," she said.

Aster just smiled and walked away.

Then Jaden reached his friends. "So what'd you think about my first duel of the year? It was pretty sweet, huh?"

"Well? Spill it!" Jaden urged.

"You rocked!" Syrus said. "Way to play, J!"

"Anyone who thinks you're a legend isn't the sharpest tack in the box," Chazz muttered.

"Maybe, but he was kind of cute," Alexis added.

"Uh, didn't notice," Jaden said. "Anyway, I'm sure we haven't seen the last of Ap."

"Hey, wait!" Syrus cried. "He said his name was A.P.!"

Syrus reached for his duelist magazine. He quickly turned the pages until he came to Aster's picture.

"He's Aster Phoenix!" Syrus said.

"Okay, so he's got a weird name," Jaden shrugged.

"Jaden, think," Alexis told him. "Aster Phoenix is the number one duelist in the World League. As in, he's a pro!"

"You're kidding me," Chazz said. "I mean, of course. You didn't know that, Jaden?"

Jaden nodded. "It looks like that pro took a schoolin'

from a student," he said, even more proud of himself than before.

"Uh, Jaden," Dorothy said. "I should probably tell you that wasn't Aster's real deck. He put it together this morning."

"He *what?*" Jaden asked. "You mean I just dueled a guy who was using leftover cards?"

"Cheer up," Syrus said.

"At least you won," Alexis added.

"That's right, you *legend* you," Chazz sneered.

Jaden smiled. "Oh yeah! You're right," he said. "And now I have a rematch to look forward to."

Jaden looked toward the Duel Academy campus.

"Hey, Aster!" he shouted. "This game is still on!"

Down at the boat docks, Crowler and Bonaparte sat forlornly next to the boat that had carried in the new students. They had waited and waited, but Aster Phoenix had not shown up.

"This doesn't make any sense," Crowler said. "He's a no-show."

"Au contraire, mon frere," Bonaparte said. "He's right there!"

Bonaparte pointed to a tall student marching down the ramp off of the boat. He didn't look a thing like Aster Phoenix. He wore a bandana over his dark brown hair. With his khaki vest and pants and tall boots, he looked like some kind of soldier. A necklace made of bones and a small animal skull hung around his neck.

The strange student marched up to Crowler and Bonaparte.

"Can you ladies tell me who's in charge around here?" he demanded.

"Ladies?" the two men protested.

"You heard me!" the student shouted. "Who's in top command of these parts?"

"That would be me," Crowler said.

The student grabbed Crowler by the collar. "I got a bone to pick!" he barked. "I'm the best duelist west of the Rio Grande! So why am I stationed in the yellow barracks? I want blue!"

"Well, you see . . ." Crowler began. Sweat poured down his pale white face. What was he supposed to say?

"What my colleague here is trying to say is that someone like you would never want to be stuck in the blue dorm," Bonaparte jumped in.

"You're too daring," Crowler said quickly. "Yes, yes. That's what it is. A thrill-seeker like you doesn't belong with the Blues."

That seemed to satisfy the student. "Well thanks," he said. Then he turned and began to march down the dock. "Left . . . left . . . left, right, left . . ."

Crowler smoothed out his frilly collar. "Who was that?" he asked.

"Beats me," Bonaparte shrugged.

"Well, that settles it," Crowler said, standing up. "This school's a joke. We need a star like Aster Phoenix, not more slackers."

"You're right!" Bonaparte agreed.

Crowler frowned. "Yes, but Aster stood us up."

"Who needs him?" Bonaparte asked. "You and I can have a whole school full of stars. All we have to do is eliminate the Red dorm. Then it's *au revoir* slackers, hello stars! Get it?"

Bonaparte's evil chuckle carried over the ocean waves. Crowler joined him.

A school without the Slifer Slackers meant a school without Jaden Yuki!

◆ CHAPTER SIX ◆

CHAZZ VS. REGINALD

Students from all over Duel Academy crowded into the school's duel arena. They filled the seats in the dome-shaped stadium.

Vice Chancellor Bonaparte stood in the center of the dueling field. Chazz stood on one side of him. On the other side stood a shorter boy in an Obelisk Blue uniform.

"Look who it is," said the boy, sneering at Chazz. "The guy who got booted from the Blues. You're going down."

"Look, kid, you're an obnoxious little punk, and I can respect that," Chazz shot back. "But no snot-nosed fresh-man can stand up to the Chazz!"

Outside, Jaden raced toward the arena. Syrus and Alexis ran with him.

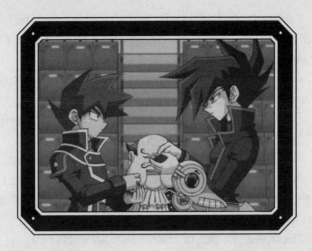

"We're gonna be late for the first official duel of the year!" Jaden cried.

"How come I've never seen you running when you're late for a class?" Syrus complained.

"Cause he saves his energy for sprinting *out* of class," Alexis said.

They ran into the arena entrance. Bonaparte was talking to the crowd with a microphone in his hand.

"Bonjour!" he said. "I'm sure by now you all know *moi!*"

"Who's the short, fat, bald guy?" Jaden asked.

"But for those of you who don't know me, I'm your Vice Chancellor, Jean Luis Bonaparte," he continued. "But enough about me. This is about him!"

Bonaparte pointed dramatically at Chazz.

"Former Obelisk Blue student Chazz Princeton," Bonaparte said. "If he wins, he goes back to the Blue dorm. Trust me, this is a duel you don't want to miss!"

The crowd clapped and cheered.

"Wow," Jaden remarked, as he and his friends walked down the aisle. "If Chazz wins this duel he gets a free pass back to Obelisk Blue."

"Yeah, but if you ask me that should have been you," Syrus said. "What boob would pick Chazz?"

Crowler blocked the aisle in front of them. "This boob!" he cried.

Syrus stepped back, surprised. "Dr. Crowler!"

"It's Chancellor Crowler now," he replied. "And there's a reason I chose Chazz for this duel. A brilliant reason, in fact."

"Somehow I doubt that," Alexis muttered.

Crowler ignored her. "Don't you slackers know who joined this year's freshman class? None other than Duelist League All-Star Aster Phoenix!"

"He enrolled here?" Alexis asked.

Jaden was eager to battle Aster again — for real. "So where is he?"

"Well, that's just it!" Crowler wailed. "For some reason, he never showed up!"

Crowler's eyes misted over with tears. His mind flashed back to the day before, when he had been so desperate to find Aster. He had sat in his office, pulling the petals off of a daisy one by one. . . .

"He loves Duel Academy. He loves us not. He loves Duel Academy. He loves us not. . . ." Crowler needed to know what was going on in Aster's mind!

Bonaparte burst into the office. "I've been looking everywhere for you!" he cried.

"What did I do to make Aster hate us?" Crowler wailed. "It's me! I've driven him away."

Then Crowler's mood quickly changed. He jumped to his feet. "Oh well, there's no sense dwelling on the past. We can't find a star, so we'll have to create one! And Chazz Princeton is the perfect candidate to launch Duel Academy into the spotlight."

"He can't be the face of our school," Bonaparte protested. "He's a Slifer Red, for Pete's sake!"

"Not for long," Crowler said. "This duel will be his chance to return to glory. You see, crowds will come rushing in to see if Chazz still has what it takes."

Crowler grinned at the brilliance of his idea.

Alexis frowned. "That's the most selfish, egotistical thing I've ever heard!"

"Thank you!" Crowler grinned.

Jaden, Syrus, and Alexis looked at one another and groaned. Crowler would never change!

They found their way to some empty seats. Down in the dueling field, Bonaparte was introducing the duelists.

"Give a big Duel Academy welcome to our challenger!" Bonaparte cried. "He's our top-ranking freshman! So give it up for Reginald Van Howell the Third!"

The crowd cheered. Chazz looked completely annoyed.

"This Reginald kid must be a pretty good duelist," Jaden remarked. "It's only his first year at the academy, and he's already in Obelisk Blue."

"No joke," Syrus agreed. "He's just like Chazz. Well, before he became a has-been."

Bonaparte continued his introduction.

"You know the drill," he told Reginald and Chazz. "No direct attacks below the belt. But trash talk is encouraged."

"Then allow me to kick off the insults!" Reginald called out in a whiny voice. "You're a nasty, stuck-up snob, and no one here likes you!"

This didn't phase Chazz at all. "I'm waiting for the insult," he replied.

Reginald looked surprised.

"Maybe you haven't picked up on this yet, little *Reggie*," Chazz taunted him. "But I do things my way. And I didn't come here to win any popularity contests!"

"Tell us something we don't know," Jaden quipped.

Bonaparte raised his arms in the air. "Now that the insults have been hurled, let's hurl some cards!" he cried.

"Sounds good!" both boys said at once. 4000 life points flashed next to each of them.

"*I'll* kick this thing off," Reginald said. "With my Marauding Captain!"

A duel monster dressed like a warrior appeared on the field. Marauding Captain wore silver armor, carried a silver sword, and had 1200 attack points.

"Now that he's on the field, I can summon another monster," Reginald continued. "Warrior Lady of the Wasteland!"

Warrior Lady had long, brown hair, and wore green boots and a tattered brown cape over a green shirt and shorts. This monster also carried a silver sword and 1100 attack points.

"Can I yawn yet?" Chazz asked. "Or do you have some more lame cards. Please tell me you're done!"

"Not by a long shot, *Chazzy*," Reginald shot back. "Check this out. I activate my Jewel Sword, and add it to my Marauding Captain!"

Reginald put a card on his Duel Disk. Marauding Captain's sword changed. Now it was much bigger, and the Captain's attack points jumped to 1500.

"But that's not my only upgrade," Reginald went on. "Next I'll boost my Warrior Lady with Divine Sword — Phoenix Blade!"

Reginald played the card, and Warrior Lady's sword transformed. Now it was larger, and the handle was shaped like a phoenix with its wings outstretched. Her attack points jumped to 1400.

Jaden and the others watched from the stands.

"Not bad!" Syrus remarked. "He's really giving Chazz a run for his money."

"Yeah, and Chazz has a ton of cash," Jaden joked.

Reginald had a smug smile on his face. "Now I'll throw down and call it a turn," he said. "Looks like you're up, Chazz Ball. Think you have what it takes? Rumor has it you own the best deck money can buy. Now let's see if it was worth it!"

• CHAPTER SEVEN •

A LEGENDARY SWORD

Reginald continued taunting Chazz.

"What's the problem? All this time as a Slifer turned you into a slacker?" he asked. "That black getup doesn't fool me. You're a redcoat, Chazz."

Chazz glared at him. "Don't you ever shut up?" he asked. "This should help. I play . . . X-Head Cannon!"

A gold cannon flashed onto the field. The Machine Monster had 1800 attack points.

"Now try this on for size!" Chazz said. He held up a card with a picture of an angelic-looking woman. "My Graceful Charity Spell card. This lets me draw three new cards as long as I ditch two."

Chazz took his three cards, then studied his deck.

"I'll start by tossing my Chthonian Polymer trap card," he said finally. "Then I'll dump Ojamagic!"

Chazz put the two cards into his graveyard.

Reginald's big eyes grew even wider. "Say wha? Oja-ma-who?"

"Am I going too fast, Reggie? Let me dumb things down for you," Chazz said. "The card is *Ojamagic!* It adds these three cards to my hand!"

Ojama Yellow appeared on the field, along with the rest of the Ojama Trio. Ojama Green had one big eye in the middle of its round head. Chubby Ojama Black had a big, bulbous nose. All three Ojamas wore skimpy red bathing suit bottoms.

"Where da party at?" the Ojama Trio cried.

"Can I attack, boss? Can I, please?" Ojama Yellow pleaded.

Across the field, Reginald frowned. "I don't get it," he said. "Why would you play three total wimps?"

"This is why!" Chazz replied, holding up the cards in his hand. "Never underestimate the power of Chazz. Now read it and weep!"

Chazz held up a new card. Reginald gasped.

"Ojama Ride!" he cried.

"I'm guessing by the stunned look on your face that you know what happens next," Chazz said, grinning. "I can summon three powerful Machine Monsters to the field as long as I scrap these three little freaks!"

"Say it ain't so!" the Ojama Trio cried. Then they vanished as Chazz banished them to his graveyard.

"Who's the slacker now, Reggie?" Chazz asked.

"Here's a hint. He's a prep-school pipsqueak. And he's in way over his dorky haircut!"

"Is it you?" Reggie asked.

"No, it's you!" Chazz shot back. "Oh, just watch. I play Y-Dragon Head!"

Chazz put the card on his Duel Disk, and a red dragon robot appeared.

"And Z-Metal Tank!" Chazz continued. A tough-looking yellow tank flashed onto the field.

"That means I can combine X, Y, and Z to form XYZ-Dragon Cannon!" Chazz shouted triumphantly.

X-Head Cannon, Y-Dragon Head, and Z-Metal Tank fused together, forming a powerful-looking machine monster. XYZ-Dragon Cannon had 2800 attack points.

"This is bad," Reginald said.

"Perceptive," Chazz said. "And it's going to get worse when I activate its special ability. By putting two cards in my graveyard I instantly send both of your monsters packing!"

Bam! Bam! A cannonball shot from each of the barrels on XYZ-Dragon Cannon. Reginald's monsters shattered right in front of him.

"Oh well. There goes your defense," Chazz said. "Dragon Cannon, direct attack!"

Boom! Now Dragon Cannon attacked Reginald directly. His life points dropped to 1200 in one shot.

"Still think you have a chance?" Chazz asked him.

Reginald scowled at Chazz. "You'll be sorry you did that to me!" he snapped. "Cause thanks to my Jewel Sword, I get to choose one card from my deck."

Reginald drew his card.

"You've got me shaking in my boots," Chazz said sarcastically.

But Reginald looked confident. "Let me show you how it's done," he said. "I activate a personal favorite of mine called Pot of Greed!"

He held up the card, showing the grinning, green face of Pot of Greed.

"Sorry! Now I get to pick up two more cards," he said.

"Stalling for time won't work, kid," Chazz told him.

"Does this look like stalling to you?" Reginald asked. He pointed to his facedown card. "I reveal Call of the Haunted, which brings a monster back from my graveyard! And I choose Warrior Lady of the Wasteland!"

Warrior Lady appeared again, her long hair waving behind her.

"And now, since I'm the kind of guy who likes to take

care of his peeps, I'm giving her a shiny new Great Sword . . . and a few more points," Reginald said.

His Warrior Lady's sword grew bigger, and her attack points jumped to 1400.

Chazz shook his head. "Well, that was pointless," he said. "It's simple math. You only raised her by three hundred! She still doesn't come close to my Dragon Cannon."

Reginald smiled. "That's exactly why I plan to sacrifice her," he said. "So I can play a little card called Gilford the Legend!"

"You're kidding," Chazz said. He sounded a little bit nervous.

"Does this look like a joke?" Reginald asked. He put a card in his Duel Disk, and a huge, muscled warrior appeared in front of him. Gilford had long hair; a mask covered half his face. He wore black armor and a brown cape. He held a massive silver sword in his arms, and 2600 attack points.

There was a murmur in the crowd of onlookers. Everyone was impressed.

"What a sweet move!" Jaden said.

Alexis nodded. "Yeah, this freshman really knows his stuff. And with that nasty 'tude, he's like a mini Chazz."

Syrus made a face. "Now that's a scary thought!"

Reginald still had more tricks up his sleeve.

"Check this out! It's time for Gilford to really strut his stuff," Reginald said. "Thanks to his special ability, he gets exclusive access to every equip spell card in my graveyard!"

Chazz let out a small gasp.

"Giving Gilford his very own Divine Sword Phoenix Blade!" Reginald cried.

Gilford's sword transformed. Now a phoenix-shaped handle glowed in Gilford's hand, and his attack points rose to 2900.

"Oh yeah, and he gets a Jewel Sword," Reginald said. Gilford's sword transformed again, now it gleamed like the sun. His attack points increased to 3200.

"And to that, I'll add a Great Sword!" Reginald cried. Gilford's sword grew even bigger, and now it was coated with shiny black metal.

His new stats were astonishing — 3500 attack points!

"How do you like my math now?" Reginald asked Chazz.

Chazz couldn't reply. He stared at Reginald's monster in shock.

But Reginald wasn't finished.

"There's more!" he announced. "I play my Flamberge Spell card. Now all I have to do is send one card to the graveyard and Gilford's sword gets even stronger!"

Reginald banished a card, and Gilford's sword grew until it nearly reached across the whole dueling arena. Fiery red flames danced on the sword's super-sharp edge.

"That sword has its own zip code!" Syrus remarked.

Jaden looked at Chazz. His eyes looked like they were popping out of his head.

"Get a load of Chazz," Jaden said. "He's bugging out!"

Syrus shuddered. "That's what a twenty-two foot flaming sword will do to a guy!"

• CHAPTER EIGHT •

OJAMA TO THE RESCUE!

"If you think this sword looks scary, watch what it can do!" Reginald called out.

"Here we go!" Jaden said.

Gilford raised the gigantic sword above his head.

Slam! The arena rocked as the sword collided with XYZ-Dragon Cannon. Chazz's massive Machine Monster exploded. His life points dropped down to 2800.

"You're defenseless!" Reginald said triumphantly.

But Chazz looked calm. "The Chazz always has a plan," he said. "So I'll play this. Look familiar?"

Chazz held up a card with a smiling green face on it.

"I have a Pot of Greed also, and it lets me draw two cards," Chazz said. He picked his cards, then smiled. "Well, what do you know? It's Ojamandala!"

A card showing the three grinning faces of the Ojama Trio appeared.

"Don't even tell me," Reginald groaned.

"I give up a thousand points to bring back you-know-who," Chazz told him.

Chazz's life points dropped to 1800. Ojama Yellow, Ojama Green, and Ojama Black flew out of the card and faced Reginald.

"These three misfits might not look like much, but they're about to take you down," Chazz warned.

"With what?" Reginald asked. He knew the Ojama Trio didn't have a single attack point between them.

"Relax, you'll see," Chazz said. As he spoke, he played another card. The card had a picture of swirling winds on it. "Time to rough them up, boys. Let's go!"

"Sure, boss!" the trio cried. They jumped into the air.

"Let's shake!" cried Ojama Yellow.

"Rattle!" said Ojama Black.

"And roll!" finished Ojama Green.

"Ojama style!" they cried together.

The three pudgy monsters flew across the field. They pounded on Gilford's chest.

"Nyah nyah nyah nyah nyah nyah!" they sang.

The powerful warrior wasn't phased at all.

Then the trio changed its strategy. They began to spin together in a circle. They spun faster and faster until they looked like a blur on the field.

"Now take him for a spin, boys!" Chazz called out.

The Ojamas dropped down over Gilford's head, circling him. They spun faster and faster until they looked like a mini tornado on the field. Dust and light covered Gilford until he couldn't be seen. Then he let out a deep cry.

Wham! Gilford the Legend vanished from the field. The Ojama Trio had just destroyed a monster with 4000 attack points!

Reginald was completely stunned. "The strongest monster in my deck . . . destroyed by dweebs . . . in undies!" he wailed.

The three Ojamas flew back to Chazz.

"They may seem like a bunch of wimps, but these three mutants can be pretty vicious," Chazz informed Reginald. "Especially when they're used with Ojama Delta Hurricane!!"

Reginald looked pretty angry. "Well, you activated the special effect of my Jewel Sword, so now I get to draw one card from my deck."

Chazz put a card face down on his disk. "I'll lay this facedown and put you out of your misery," he told Reginald.

"Wait, let me guess. That's another Ojama card, right?" Reginald asked.

"Why'd you say that?" Chazz asked.

"Oh, I don't know. Maybe because you built your entire deck around those three stooges!" Reginald replied. "I've had it! Those freaks have made a fool out of me for the last time."

"You're right, kid," Chazz shot back. "Why let them make a fool out of you when you do such a great job of making a fool out of yourself?"

"Whatever," Reginald sneered. "You're a second-rate duelist with a third-rate deck. Now watch . . . and learn!"

Reginald held up a card. "See this? It's called a *real* card. And once I pay 800 points, a monster comes back from my grave. And I choose Armed Samurai — Ben Kei!"

Reginald's life points dropped down to 400. Then a Warrior appeared on the field. Ben Kei had a white scarf draped over the top of his head. He carried a basket of weapons on his back. 500 attack points flashed next to him.

"But wait! I'm not done!" Reginald continued. "Next I'll remove two Warriors from the game! And it's all thanks to the special ability of my Divine Sword — Phoenix Blade card."

Reginald put two of his cards in his back pocket.

"Now there's one thing left to do," Reginald said. "I take Lightning Blade and Divine Sword and give them to Samurai Ben Kei!"

Reginald put two cards in his Duel Disk. Lightning Sword appeared in Ben Kei's left hand. His attack points jumped to 800. Then the shining Divine Sword appeared in his right hand, and his attack points jumped all the way up to 1600.

"Now attack! Destroy that yellow pipsqueak!" Reginald shouted.

Ben Kei jumped across the field. He raised the Divine Sword, then brought it down on Ojama Yellow.

"Oh noooooo!" the little yellow monster cried.

Then he vanished.

"You're not in the clear yet, Chazz," Reginald said. "My Samurai gets an extra attack for every card he's equipped with."

"What?" Chazz was stunned.

In the stands, Jaden had it all figured out. "Do the math. Reggie gets three more attacks," he said. "And Chazz has two more monsters. . . . No, seriously, somebody do the math for me."

Reginald grinned as he called for the destruction of the rest of the Ojama Trio.

"One!" he shouted.

Ben Kei brought his mighty sword down on Ojama Black.

"Two!"

The samurai slashed at Ojama Green.

Chazz knew the third attack was coming. He could take the damage himself. Or . . .

Decision time, Chazz told himself. *If I activate my trap card now I'll block his direct attack. But I'll also lose one of my Ojama cards.*

He took a deep breath. *Oh well. No pain, no gain.*

He decided not to activate the trap card yet. He faced Ben Kei, gritting his teeth.

Wham! The samurai's sword hit Chazz directly. His life points dropped from 1800 to 200 in one blow.

"Strike three. You're out," Reginald said smugly.

Chazz's dark eyes glared at Reginald.

"Aw, what's wrong?" Reginald asked. "You miss your little friends? Loogey, Mucus, and Snot Ball?"

"They're not my friends," Chazz said. "But I'll bring them back anyway!"

"What?" Reginald thought he was done with the Ojama Trio for good.

Now Chazz played his trap card.

"My Ojama Delta Wear card automatically returns the gruesome trio to the field!" Chazz cried.

The three monsters flew out of the card. They sobbed dramatically.

"I bet ya missed us!" they cried.

"He likes us! He really likes us!" bawled Ojama Green.

Tears streamed from Ojama Yellow's bulging eyes. "Oh happy day!"

Reginald shook his head, disgusted. "Ah, Team Pathetic is reunited," he said. "And guess who the biggest loser of them all is?"

"I'm sure you're about to tell me," Chazz said dryly.

"It's you!" Reginald cried, pointing at Chazz. "And you'll never be Blue again!"

• CHAPTER NINE •

CHAZZ IT UP!

"How does it feel to be a Slifer 'Lifer'?" Reginald asked Chazz.

"You know, I used to be just like you," Chazz replied. "An elitist snob who looked down on everyone around me. But I've changed. Know how? Now I'm a snob who only looks down on *some* people."

Jaden grinned. At least Chazz was being honest. But he wondered how Chazz was going to win the duel with only 200 life points to spare.

"Anyway, there's a lesson here. I'm just . . . not sure where," Chazz said. He pumped his fist in the air. "Now I merge my Ojamas together to form Ojama King!"

The Ojama Trio swirled together. A bright light

flashed. When it faded, a huge Ojama monster towered over the field. Ojama King had a huge, gray head that sat on top of a tiny body. Its eyeballs dangled on the end of two long eyestalks. It wore one red bathing suit on its bottom, and another on top of its head — underneath a crown, of course.

"Thank you. Thank you very much," Ojama King said.

"Dude, your King has no points!" Reginald pointed out.

"Gee, thanks," Chazz replied. "It's a good thing he won't be around much longer, cause I'm activating this!"

Chazz held up a card. "Mecha Ojama King Transformation!" he cried.

Ojama King jumped high in the air. When it bounced back onto the field, it had been transformed into a mecha — a mechanical Ojama King. Its whole body was made of metal. But it still had zero attack points.

Reginald frowned. "But that doesn't make any — "

"Yeah, I know. You're wondering why my Mecha Ojama King doesn't have any attack points either," Chazz said.

Mecha Ojama King chuckled.

"What he does have is a special ability to let me summon one Ojamachine with each turn," Chazz said, and Reginald cringed. Chazz selected his card. "I play Ojamachine Yellow!"

A little monster that looked like a robot Ojama Yellow appeared on the field.

"Did I mention this little geek-bot has a cool party trick of his own?" Chazz asked.

Ojamachine Yellow opened up its mouth — and another Ojamachine Yellow jumped out!

That Ojamachine opened its mouth — and another Ojamachine Yellow jumped out next!

Then a fourth Ojamachine Yellow jumped out of the mouth of the third Ojamachine.

"Now listen up, little dudes," bellowed Mecha Ojama King. "Hop to it!"

"Attack!" Chazz yelled.

Ojamachine Yellow and the three Tokens hopped across the field.

"This is insane!" Reginald cried out. "My Samurai has sixteen hundred points! Your toads have zero."

The first Ojamachine Yellow jumped onto Gilford the Legend's armored chest.

Poof! The little monster vanished.

"Yes, I win!" Reginald cheered.

"Actually, it's the opposite," Chazz told him. "When my Ojamachine Yellow is destroyed, my points don't change. But I can't say the same for yours, 'cause you're about to take three hundred points of damage!"

Reginald gaped helplessly as his points dropped from 400 to 100.

"That means . . ." Reginald stammered.

"Spit it out, Reggie," Chazz said. "It means one more attack and you lose!"

Reginald gasped. His face turned pale. He knew Chazz was right.

Chazz grinned. "Welcome to Duel Academy, freshman."

"Get him, boys!" Mecha Ojama King yelled.

The three Ojamachine Yellow tokens happily hopped into Gilford the Legend.

Slam! Slam! Slam! All the monsters vanished.

And Reginald was left with no life points at all. He fell to his knees.

Chazz walked toward him. "It looks like slumming with the Slifers hasn't hurt my game," he said. "Maybe now you'll see that the color of your coat doesn't mean squat. 'Cause an Obelisk Blue, who's supposed to be the best of the best, just got schooled by a Slifer Red!"

Chazz looked down at Reginald. "Face it, kid. Whether you're wearing blue, yellow, red, or polka dots, you'll always be the same loser, and I'll always be the Chazz!"

The crowd erupted in cheers and applause. Chazz raised his arms in triumph.

"Chazz it up! Chazz it up! Chazz it up!" everyone chanted.

Chancellor Crowler was delighted. This was exactly the victory he had been hoping for.

"Chazz it up! Chazz it up!" he chanted with the crowd.

Bonaparte looked up at him, scowling.

"The Chazz has spoken!" Chazz announced.

Jaden was so excited, he ran down onto the dueling field.

"Way to win one for the Reds," he said. He gripped Chazz in a bear hug. "I always knew you were one of us!"

Chazz looked horrified. "I never said that!"

The other Slifer Red students ran onto the field, too.

"Three big Slifer cheers for Chazz!" one of them yelled.

All the boys picked up Chazz. They tossed him into the air.

"Slifer! Slifer! Slifer!" they chanted.

Chazz frantically waved his arms. "Drop me, you dorks! I'm not one of you!"

But the excited Slifers ignored him.

Crowler and Bonaparte made their way onto the field.

"I didn't see this coming," Crowler admitted. "But if he wants to be a slacker, who am I to stop him?"

The Slifer students dropped Chazz. Luckily, Jaden and Syrus reached in and caught him.

Crowler spoke into a microphone.

"Attention, please!" he called out. "There's been a change of plans. Chazz Princeton shall remain in Slifer Red!"

Chazz panicked. That wasn't what his speech had been about at all!

"But I don't want — " he tried to explain, but Crowler interrupted him.

"There's no need to thank me," he said. "I'm just doing my job."

"At this rate it won't be your job very much longer," Bonaparte muttered.

"Chazz it up! Chazz it up! Chazz it up!" the Slifers cheered.

"Will you all shut up!" Chazz screamed.

Jaden put his arm around Chazz. "Hey, now that you're our team mascot we've got a ton of stuff to do. Fit you for a red jacket, teach you the secret handshake . . ."

The rest of the day continued as normal. Syrus was walking back from a class when he passed Crowler's office. He heard loud voices coming from inside.

"But this makes an even better story for the press," Crowler was saying.

"Forget about the press," Bonaparte snapped. "If you want this school to rise to greatness, there needs to be some changes. I told you, we need to bid the Slifers *adieu!*"

Crowler was surprised. "You were serious?"

"I don't kid, Crowler," Bonaparte said darkly. "It's high time we tear down the Slifer dorm!"

"Tear down the Slifer dorm?" Syrus cried. Panicked, he ran to the dorm as fast as he could. He found Jaden in the room they shared and told him what he'd heard.

"Are you positive?" Jaden asked.

Syrus nodded. "They want to get rid of us," he said nervously. "I'm telling you, I saw this in a movie once. These guys in dark suits show up. Then they tell us we're going to 'sleep with the fishes' and no one hears from us again!"

Suddenly, the building began to shake.

"Oh no! Too late!" Jaden cried.

"You're right!" Syrus wailed. "We're gonna get exterminated!"

Jaden and Syrus ran outside to the deck. They saw Chazz standing in front of the building.

"Run, Chazz!" Jaden cried.

"They're here!" Syrus warned.

Chazz rolled his eyes. "What are you dorks talking about? These guys are building a private room onto this dump."

Chazz pointed to the right of the building, where workmen had erected some scaffolding. The "room" was twice as big as the Slifer dorm!

"I figure if I'm stuck in this place, I may as well be living in style," Chazz said.

Jaden turned to Syrus. "So much for your theory."

"I guess I got a little carried away," Syrus admitted. "Sorry for the scare."

"I guess we should lay off those late night movies for a while," Jaden said. He looked out over the campus.

Syrus had a pretty big imagination. But he believed his friend had heard something outside Crowler's office.

I wonder if what Syrus overheard is true, Jaden thought, worried. *Do they really want to tear down our dorm?*

• CHAPTER TEN •

THE BULLY ON THE BRIDGE

"This is so unchill!" Jaden complained. He and Syrus were walking along a wooded path. Jaden had a bunch of Duel Disks strapped to his back. Syrus struggled to carry a heavy net that held several disks.

"I sleep through one of Crowler's boring lectures and he makes us lug fourteen replacement Duel Disks across campus," Jaden went on. "Why's everyone losing theirs, anyway?"

"Well . . ." Syrus began. He had an uncomfortable look on his face.

"You know something, don't you," Jaden said. "Come on, spill it!"

Syrus stopped walking and rested the sack on the ground. "I don't know for sure," he said carefully. "But I've heard things. You know the West River? Over by the main bridge?"

"Yeah, what about it?" Jaden asked.

"Well, there's this bully who hangs out over there," Syrus said. "Uh, so I hear. And he forces you to duel him . . . so I'm told."

Jaden was getting impatient. "Yeah? And?"

"And if you lose, his gang takes your Duel Disk away!" Syrus told him. He was trembling now.

Jaden shook his head. This guy at the bridge sounded like a real jerk.

"What else do you know? Come on!" Jaden asked.

"I'm just telling you what I heard," Syrus insisted. "He might not even exist. For all I know, this guy is just a myth — the big, ugly muscle head."

Jaden paused. Was Syrus trying to tell him something? He looked at his friend.

"Hey, where's your Duel Disk?" he asked.

Syrus blushed. "Well . . ."

"Sy! Did you duel this guy and lose?" Jaden asked.

"Yes!" Syrus admitted. "And he took my lunch money, too!"

Jaden began to quickly walk down the path. "In that case, I say we take the long way home," he called back behind him.

"Wait!" Syrus cried, running to catch up. "Do you mean —"

"I sure do!" Jaden replied. "Come on. We've got some Duel Disks to win back!"

Syrus shook his head. "Oh boy. I was afraid he'd do this," he muttered. Then he took off after Jaden.

It didn't take them long to get to the West River. As they got closer to the river bank, they saw a tall boy standing in the center of the bridge. It was the same student who had roughed up Crowler on the first day of school, but Jaden didn't know that. All he knew was that the boy had on a pretty strange outfit.

The bandana covering his dark brown hair had the face of a dinosaur on it. White dinosaur teeth jutted out from under the bandana. He wore khaki pants, and he had cut off the sleeves of his Ra Yellow jacket.

"Stop right there, civilians!" the boy ordered them.

"That's him, Jaden," Syrus said nervously. "That's the guy. Maybe we should go! Who needs lunch money, anyway?"

As Syrus talked, five guys wearing cut-off Ra Yellow jackets walked up behind the bully. They stood on either side of him. They all wore dino-faced bandanas.

"Draw your Duel Disk!" the bully demanded.

Jaden grinned. "Sure," he said. He slid the Duel Disks off of his back so he could reach his own.

The bully looked confused. "Hold on. Aren't you scared?"

"Of a duel?" Jaden asked. "No way! Now let's throw down!"

"But I haven't given my speech yet," the bully complained.

"What speech?" Jaden asked.

"My intro!" the boy said. "Now then. Name's Hassleberry. Code name: Tyranno!"

Jaden shrugged. "Whatever you say." He nodded toward the boys gathered around Hassleberry. "What's with the goon squad?"

"Show some respect!" Hassleberry barked.

"That's right!" said one of the goons, a tall, heavy boy. "You tell 'em, Sarge!"

The smallest goon, a short boy with brown hair, held

a red megaphone to his lips. "Like, state your name," he called out.

"Well, I — " Jaden began.

" — was just leaving!" Syrus said, tugging on Jaden's sleeve.

The short goon shouted through the megaphone again. "Roll call time!"

"Who are we?" shouted the big goon.

"Troop Tyranno!" all the boys shouted together. One of the squad waved a flag with a dinosaur face on it.

Jaden shook his head. "Okay. They're nuts."

"That's what scares me," Syrus said.

The boys marched around the bridge.

"Sound off! Ready?" cried one boy. "Sarge Tyranno is the best!"

"He likes to wear his jacket as a vest!" answered another boy. "Sound off, one two!"

"Sound off, three four!" yelled the big goon. "Now let's go!"

The short squad member squinted at Syrus. "Hold on! You look like the kid whose undies we hung on the flagpole yesterday."

"What's the point?" Syrus asked, clenching his fists.

"Does it really matter?" Jaden asked. He was itching to duel. "Let's just throw down!"

"Well first, let me lay down the rules of battle," Hassleberry said. He pointed to the replacement Duel Disks Jaden had placed on the ground. "You see those Duel Disks? You lose, them things is mine."

"And if I win, you give me the ones you stole!" Jaden shot back.

Hassleberry looked surprised. "Say what?"

"Who *are* you?" the Tyranno squad asked. Nobody had ever challenged Hassleberry before.

"Just another wimp," Hassleberry said.

Syrus forgot his fear. "Hey, take that back!" he said, stepping forward. "Hear me? No one insults my best friend!"

Hassleberry frowned. "Control your subordinate, will ya?" he told Jaden.

"Yeah!" echoed Troop Tyranno.

"Or else we will," said the short goon.

"Forget that pipsqueak," said the tallest squad member. "Eyes on the prize!"

"When I'm done with this run, they'll have to scrape him off the ground with a squeegee," Hassleberry promised.

Troop Tyranno began to hoot and holler.

"Way to go, Sarge!"

"Look at that civilian squirm!"

Hassleberry dramatically pointed at Jaden.

"All right!" he cried. "You got a deal. And a duel!"

• CHAPTER ELEVEN •

TIME FOR COMBAT!

Jaden and Hassleberry took their places for the duel. They each stood on one side of the river. Syrus climbed up on the bridge with Troop Tyranno.

"Are you always this dramatic, bro?" Jaden called out to Hassleberry.

Over on the bridge, Syrus was getting into the fighting spirit.

"Atteeention!" he yelled. "Time for combat, Sarge!"

Jaden looked at his friend and shook his head. "Clearly you're not the only dramatic one," he remarked.

"Ready for boot camp, son?" Hassleberry yelled.

"Hey you!" Syrus called from the bridge. "Stop calling him 'son.' Jaden's in his second year!"

"Then he's number *two*!" said the short squad member.

"And who's number one?" the big guy asked.

"Troop Tyranno!" the boys cried.

Syrus turned to them, annoyed. "Will you give it up? You're not in the army!"

This only got Troop Tyranno all riled up. They whipped out a bunch of horns and drums. They began to honk and thump them.

"Who's the best? Troop Tyranno!" they cried. "And who's gonna win?"

"Troop Jaden!" Syrus yelled.

Jaden sighed. "Am I the only one who's not going insane?"

"Rally up!" Hassleberry called to his troops. "All hands on deck!"

"Well, he just answered *that* question loud and clear," Jaden quipped. He took out his deck of cards and inserted it into his Duel Disk. "Fine. If you can't beat them, you gotta join them. Game on, General!"

Hassleberry's beady eyes narrowed. "You mocking me?" he asked. "I'm a sergeant, junior! And this ain't no game. This is combat!"

Hassleberry activated his Duel Disk, too.

"All right, then, get your combat on!" Jaden said. "Ready, Chief? I declare war. By summoning Elemental Hero Wildheart in defense mode!"

Elemental Hero Wildheart had a brown, muscled body and long black hair. Streaks of war paint decorated the hero's face and arms. He knelt next to Jaden, and had 1600 defense points.

"Now I'll call it a turn," Jaden finished.

"Who's the best? Troop Jaden!" Syrus cheered.

Troop Tyranno began to bang their drums and honk their horns again.

"You call that a cheer? Well step to the rear!" they chanted.

Hassleberry was ready to make his move.

"Trench warfare time!" he announced. "Here goes! Gilasaurus, front and center!"

A dark green dinosaur appeared on the field. Gilasaurus walked on two legs. It roared loudly, revealing a mouth full of sharp teeth. The monster had 1400 attack points.

Syrus winced. Gilasaurus looked pretty tough. "Well, it could be worse," he said hopefully.

"And now things are about to get a lot worse," Hassleberry said. "Cause that right there was a special summon. Which, in layman's turns, means I can play *another* monster! So Gilasaurus, you are dismissed. Now Dark Driceratops, report to the field in attack mode!"

Gilasaurus vanished, and a new dino appeared in its place. Dark Driceratops had a green, leathery body. Sharp purple claws extended from its arms and feet. Feathered wings grew from its back, and purple feathers crowned the top of its head. The monster boasted an impressive 2400 attack points.

Jaden was definitely impressed. "Not bad!" he said sincerely. "You played a monster with 2400 attack points in your first turn!"

"This is war!" Syrus shouted. "Don't give the enemy any props!"

"It's time to go commando," Hassleberry said. "Dark Driceratops, attack! Flying Phantom Nose Dive!"

Driceratops jumped up and flew across the river.

Slam! It collided into Wildheart, shattering the warrior into pieces.

But there was more. Driceratops flew up again, but this time, it headed toward Jaden.

Wham! The heavy dino smacked into Jaden, sending him falling to his knees. His life points dropped down to 3200.

Hassleberry chuckled. "At ease, private!" he cried.

• CHAPTER TWELVE •

JURASSIC WORLD!

"You okay, Jay?" Syrus asked anxiously.

"Get up, son," Hassleberry ordered Jaden. "My prehistoric patrol isn't through with you yet! But since I'm nice, I'll give you a chance to recoup. But not for long. I'll be layin' on the hurt soon enough!"

Jaden struggled to get back to his feet. Hassleberry grinned.

"That's what you get when you mess with the best!" he said proudly.

Troop Tyranno sprang into action.

"Hassleberry, Hassleberry, he's our man! If he can't win — "

"*We* will!" Syrus finished for them. "Now take it down a decibel."

The short goon aimed the megaphone right in Syrus's face. "Sorry, little man, but the Sarge needs support! If it's too loud, then get lost!"

Syrus winced at the loud noise. He turned to Jaden.

"Beat the khaki pants off this guy so we can shut them up!" he yelled.

"What do you think I'm trying to do? Let him win?" Jaden yelled back. He nodded at Hassleberry. "Hey, Lieutenant. My move!"

"For the last time, it's *sergeant!*" Hassleberry replied, annoyed. "Now play something!"

Jaden looked through the cards in his hand. He held one up.

"Monster Reincarnation!" he announced. "I'll send this to the graveyard in order to bring back my Wildheart. How do you like that?"

Hassleberry laughed. "You want that wimp in your platoon?"

"Negative," Jaden answered. "But I do want this in my graveyard."

He banished a card, and as he spoke, the spectre of a red monster with large claws appeared behind Jaden.

Hassleberry gasped. "Sam Hill!" he cried. "That's Necroshade!"

"Bingo!" Jaden answered. "And I'm guessing you know what *that* means, right, Captain? That I can automatically summon this . . ."

Jaden held up a card. A shining gold Hero monster appeared on the field in front of him. The hero's muscled body looked like a carved gold statue. Gold horns curled on top of its head, and bright, blue eyes shone from its face.

"Elemental Hero Bladedge!" Jaden cried. This monster had 2600 attack points. "Go, Bladedge! Attack his Dark Driceratops! Slice and Dice attack!"

Bladedge raced across the river and slammed into Driceratops with incredible force. *Bam!* The dino monster exploded in a ball of fire. Hassleberry shielded himself from the blast as his own life points dropped down to 3800.

"That should do for now," Jaden said, smiling. He had destroyed a massive monster *and* damaged Hassleberry in one turn. Not bad.

"Awesome! Way to play, Jay!" Syrus cheered.

"Thanks, Sy," Jaden replied.

Syrus turned to Troop Tyranno. They weren't cheering now.

"So you're speechless now, huh?" Syrus taunted them.

Hassleberry frowned. *This civilian ain't that bad,* he thought to himself. *But the sergeant still has a few tactics up his sleeve. . . .*

Troop Tyranno let out a weak cheer. "Rah, rah rah. Go Sarge . . ." they said.

Hassleberry sighed. His boys tried so hard. He didn't want to let them down. He thought about the events that had brought him to this bridge. . . .

"When I first tried out for Duel Academy, I had my eyes on the Obelisk Blues," Hassleberry muttered to himself. "And when I aced my exam, I thought I was a shoo-in! So when they stuck me in the Yellow barracks, I thought they made a tactical error.

"Turns out you had to go to a fancy prep school to be a Blue," Hassleberry continued. "So I made do, and just like my daddy told me I would, I emerged as a true commanding officer. Before long I formed a squadron. My soldiers. My platoon! My battalion!"

Hassleberry's eyes misted over. "And we let it be known that Sergeant Tyranno Hassleberry, son of the great General Hassleberry, is a giant among men! A dino-man! And I guard this bridge to prove that no matter what, I will not stand down!"

Hassleberry didn't realize it, but he was now shouting across the dueling field.

"Enough with the monologue," Syrus said, laughing. "Get back to the duel already!"

Hassleberry looked embarrassed. "Was I thinkin' out loud again?"

Troop Tyranno nodded.

"You're a pretty funny guy, Bumble-berry," Jaden said.

"It's Hassleberry!" his opponent snapped. "Sergeant Hassleberry!"

Hassleberry took a deep breath. "Now back to the battle," he said. He looked at his deck. "Excellent! *Terrain* advantage! I play this."

He put a card in his disk. The ground began to shake.

"It's a field spell card known as Jurassic World!" Hassleberry said proudly.

The scene all around them changed. The river and bridge disappeared, replaced by green grass and tropical-looking trees. A volcano belched smoke in the background.

"Jurassic World? No way," Jaden said, impressed. "Pretty sweet move."

"You ain't seen nothin', soldier," Hassleberry told him. "Now get this. Every one of my dinos and winged beasts gains 300 attack and defense points. Not only that, but they can't be affected by any of your trap cards. And not only that . . ."

Jaden's eyes widened. There was more?

"If my monsters happen to be attacked while in attack mode, then they have the right to dig into the trenches and switch themselves into defense mode," Hassleberry continued.

"Now that's what I call a major advantage!" Syrus said, worried.

"It's battle time!" Hassleberry cried out. He put a

card in his disk. "Archeonys, report for duty! In attack mode, of course."

A Winged Beast with blue feathers appeared in front of Hassleberry. Yellow feathers lined the bottom of its wings. Its orange beak held scary-looking sharp teeth. It had 300 attack points.

"Thanks to my Jurassic World, my monster gains 300 more attack points," Hassleberry reminded Jaden.

Syrus did the math. "Only 600 points?" he said. "Bladedge can beat that!"

"But Bladedge isn't the target," Hassleberry said. He looked at Jaden. "*You* are, private! Archeonys can attack your life points directly!"

Syrus gasped.

Hassleberry pointed to his Winged Beast. "Now! Debilitate the enemy with Screamin' Eagle Attack!"

◄ • CHAPTER THIRTEEN • ►

BLACK TYRANNO!

Archeonys flapped its huge wings and flew across the field. It opened its beak and let out an unearthly cry. The sonic waves from the scream slammed into Jaden.

"Now drop and give me 600! 600 life points, that is," Hassleberry said.

Jaden grimaced as his life points dropped down to 2600.

Hassleberry grinned. "I'll place one card face down and defer to you," he told Jaden. "Face it, son. It's over. Before long, you'll be extinct. Wouldn't you agree, squadron?"

Hassleberry waited for the cheers of Troop Tyranno. But none came. He turned his head, and saw that most of his squad was now sitting on the Jurassic grass. "You men were supposed to cheer just now," Hassleberry said.

The big goon shrugged. "Right, uh, sorry. We were moved internally. We'll have an outward display next time, sir."

One of the squad members yawned.

"Yeah, and we'll cheer for you, too," the short boy added helpfully.

Hassleberry frowned. "What am I gonna do with you?"

"Hey, major?" Jaden called out. "Keep those eyes on the prize, okay? Ready? I play my Elemental Hero Wildheart in attack mode!"

Wildheart appeared again, flexing his muscles. He had 1500 attack points.

The short goon held his megaphone right up to Syrus's face. "That's really strange," he boomed. "Why would he play that Wild — "

"My ears!" Syrus wailed.

The boy sheepishly put down the megaphone. "Whoops," he said. "I mean, like why would he play that Wildheart again?"

"Here's the deal," Syrus replied. "Jaden's the best. You just don't question his strategies."

"Ooooh," said Troop Tyranno. They were impressed.

"This is insubordination!" Hassleberry fumed.

Jaden tried to ignore all the dramatics. He had a duel to fight.

"All right, Bladedge!" he called to his golden hero. "Destroy his Archeonys now! Slice and Dice Attack!"

Bladedge charged across the field, but Hassleberry's trap card flipped up. Bladedge stopped.

"I'm fortified with this!" Hassleberry announced. "Amber Pitfall! It deflects an attacking monster and forces it into defense mode!"

A wave of golden amber poured from the card. It splashed into Bladedge, pushing him back next to Jaden. Bladedge knelt in defense mode, with 1800 defense points.

"Now he's gotta stay like that," Hassleberry said. "That means no more offensive maneuvers from now on!"

Jaden smiled. "But you're forgetting something," he said. "I still have Wildheart!"

Jaden pointed to his hero. "Now attack with Wild Slash!"

Wildheart drew the heavy metal sword he kept strapped to his back. He flew across the field, his sword raised, ready to strike Archeonys.

"Now *you're* forgetting something," Hassleberry told him. "My field spell card. When my feathered friend is attacked, he has the option of switching to defense mode!"

Archaeonys switched to Defense. The Winged Beast had 1300 defense points.

"What's the point?" Jaden asked. Wildheart had 1500 attack points. Archeonys would be destroyed either way.

"The point is, it survives!" Hassleberry replied.

"But Jaden's monster is still stronger," Syrus pointed out.

"Not exactly, little man," Hassleberry told him. "Mine gets a defense point boost!"

Thanks to Jurassic World, Archeonys's defense points rose to 1600.

Wildheart lowered his sword. He had no choice — he had to finish the attack.

But the blue bird was stronger than him now. Wildheart's sword came down — and shattered. Jaden's life points took the rest of the damage, and dropped down to 2500.

Jaden didn't seem bothered at all by losing both his heroes.

"I'll throw down two facedowns and call it a turn," he said, smiling. "That'll teach me. Oh well. Live and learn."

One of the Tyranno boys scratched his head. "That's weird."

"He's *smiling*," said another boy, in disbelief.

"Jaden always has a good time," Syrus told them. "Unlike the sarge."

Troop Tyranno laughed, and Hassleberry frowned.

My battalion is deserting me, he thought. *This always happens. I find a troop of soldiers I can trust and they end up siding with the enemy!*

Oh well. He would show them.

"No more Mr. Nice Sarge!" he growled. "Now brace yourself, 'cause I play this. My Earthquake spell card!"

Hassleberry held up the card, and the ground began to shake. A huge crack opened up in the earth, stretching across the field until it reached Wildheart's feet. He fell to his knees, and 1600 defense points flashed next to him.

"Now every face up monster on the field is forced into defense mode!" Hassleberry announced.

Jaden struggled to keep his balance until the earthquake quieted down.

"I'm far from done!" Hassleberry threatened. He held up another card. "Ultra Evolution! This card lets me reverse the whole evolutionary process. So I'll just sacrifice one of my Winged Beasts to summon a dino."

Hassleberry noticed the curious look on Jaden's face.

"You see, they say some birds evolved from dinosaurs," he explained.

"Really?" Jaden asked.

Hassleberry nodded. "Yup. So when Archeonys undergoes reverse evolution, it becomes a dinosaur!"

Jaden watched in amazement as the feathered monster vanished, and a towering dinosaur appeared in its place. Black Tyranno had yellow stripes on its thick, black skin. It roared loudly over the field, waving its sharp claws. An awesome 2600 attack points flashed next to it. Then the attack points jumped to 2900, thanks to Jurassic World.

"A Black Tyranno, to be exact!" Hassleberry said proudly. "And surprise! Thanks to my dino's special ability, it can attack you directly!"

Jaden gasped. He only had 2500 life points left.

Black Tyranno was about to turn him into toast!

• CHAPTER FOURTEEN •

A NEW HERO

"All right, Black Tyranno!" Hassleberry shouted. "You're on! Now sic 'em!"

The huge dino monster stomped across the field. The ground shook as if Hassleberry had used an Earthquake card. Clouds of dust billowed up from the ground, covering the field like a fog.

With a load roar, Tyranno lifted a massive leg and stomped right down on Jaden.

"Mission accomplished!" Hassleberry said confidently.

But when the dust cleared, Jaden and his heroes were still standing. Jaden still had 100 life points left.

Hassleberry's eyes widened with surprise. "How is it you still have life points, boy?"

"I activated my facedown card, Insurance!" Jaden replied. The card floated in the air in front of him. "It takes one facedown trap or spell card on the field and returns it to my hand. And when Insurance returns to my hand, my life points increase by five hundred!"

Hassleberry was confused. The Insurance card was right in front of him! "But it's on the *field*," he pointed out. "Not in your hand, son!"

Jaden grinned. "That's true. But I've got two Insurance cards!"

He turned around the card in his hand to show Hassleberry. The dino-obsessed duelist groaned.

Jaden had played that move perfectly. By putting down two Insurance cards facedown on his last turn, he had guaranteed himself an extra 500 points. It was just enough to keep him alive in the duel.

"Nice one, Jay!" Syrus called out.

Even Troop Tyranno was impressed.

"Sergeant Jaden is the best!" chanted the short squad member.

Hassleberry sighed. "Deserted. Again," he said sadly. "It's nothin' new. Guess the only person I can trust is me. It's always the same. I gather a battalion of supporters, and when I need 'em most, they just desert me."

Hassleberry sat on the ground, deep in thought. "But why?" he wondered out loud. "I'm a great leader and I always win. Who wouldn't want to root for me? Take this duel. I'm beating you the same way I beat my last twelve rivals."

"Well, colonel, maybe they're just bored," Jaden suggested.

Hassleberry looked up. "Bored with my duelin'? That's just crazy talk," he replied.

"Think about it, Dingleberry," Jaden said. "You said yourself you've used the same moves for twelve duels in a row. So don't you think it's time you evolved?"

"Nice dinosaur reference, Jay!" Syrus cheered.

"Ditto!" said the big squad member.

Troop Tyranno nodded in agreement.

"I'm not bored anymore!" cried the smallest one.

Hassleberry couldn't believe it. "You were right," he told Jaden.

"I always am," Jaden said. "Now to prove it. Ready? I play Pot of Greed. So I can draw two cards."

Jaden took two new cards from his deck. He smiled.

"Now getting back to this whole evolution thing, I play this!" He held up a card with tall buildings on it. "My own field spell card! Sorry, but the Stone Age is over."

All around them, Jurassic World began to change. First, a sheet of ice covered everything in a deep freeze.

"Is this the Ice Age?" Hassleberry asked in wonder.

"Just wait," Jaden said. "The field's still evolving."

The earth below their feet rumbled as tall skyscrapers rose up from the ground. Soon the buildings towered above them. Stars flickered in the night sky that covered the field.

"My spell card is called Skyscraper and it changes everything," Jaden explained.

"I hate change!" Hassleberry cried. "You hear me!"

Then Hassleberry stopped, struck by the sound of his own words.

That's been my problem all along, he realized. *I've been stuck in the past, always relying on the same old tactics, instead of learning from my mistakes and evolving!*

"Exactly!" Jaden said, grinning. "Don't worry, corporal. You weren't thinking out loud this time. But I assumed by the look on your face that you figured it out."

Jaden got ready to finish up the duel.

"Now since your field card is gone, so are three hundred of Black Tyranno's attack points!" Jaden reminded Hassleberry. The dino's points dropped down to 2600.

"And if you like that, you'll love this, 'cause it's time for some fusion action," Jaden said. He held up two cards: Elemental Hero Avian and Polymerization.

"I merge Elemental Hero Avian with Elemental Hero Wildheart in order to create my newest hero!" Jaden announced. He put the cards in his Duel Disk. "Elemental Hero Wild Wingman!"

Avian and Wildheart swirled together. A bright light

flashed, and a new hero stood in their place. Wild Wingman had Wildheart's muscled body and Avian's huge, white wings. And this monster had 1900 attack points.

"He's got a pretty sweet side effect," Jaden promised. "If I toss a card, your trap is automatically destroyed!"

Hassleberry gasped as his trap card shattered into pieces.

"And now that your Amber Pitfall is gone, I can switch Bladedge to attack mode!" Jaden cried. Bladedge stood up, boasting 2800 attack points once again.

"You don't say?" Hassleberry responded.

Syrus turned to Troop Tyranno. "Ready, boys? Make some noise!"

"Jaden! Jaden! Jaden!" they chanted.

And Jaden was far from finished. "Thanks to my Skyscraper card, Wild Wingman's attack points increase by a thousand," he said. Now Wild Wingman had 2900 points. "Okay, Wingman, get your attack on! Wing Impulse!"

Wild Wingman flew up and flapped his wings. Sonic waves poured out from them, slamming into Black Tyranno. The huge dino monster exploded from the impact.

Hassleberry took the rest of the damage and his life points dropped to 3500.

"That's not all," Jaden said. "There's Bladedge. And he can attack you directly!"

"Oh boy," Hassleberry said.

Bladedge leapt up and zoomed across the field.

Whack! He pummeled Hassleberry with a martial

arts kick. The sergeant's life points plummeted down to 900.

"Troop Jaden rocks!" chanted the former Troop Tyranno.

Hassleberry firmly faced Jaden. "I've still got 900 life points left. Close. But no medal for you."

But Jaden held up another card. A nervous look crossed Hassleberry's face.

"I'm not finished. I still have this," Jaden told him. "De-fusion! So Wildheart and Avian can separate. Which means each of them can attack now. So there go your life points!"

Wild Wingman separated back into the two heroes, Wildheart with his 1000 attack points, and Avian with 1500 attack points.

Hassleberry knew what was coming. But strangely, he wasn't upset. This duel was one of the best he'd fought in a long time.

"Go, Avian, Quill Cascade!" Jaden cried.

He smiled calmly and braced himself for the attack. He gritted his teeth as sharp feathers flew from Avian's wings, decimating his life points.

"What a battle," Hassleberry said, as the feathers flew. "Jaden, you've got spirit, soldier."

Hassleberry's life points dropped to zero. The effect of the field card stopped, and the field transformed back to the West River once again. But Hassleberry didn't realize it.

"I got to hand it to you, son," Hassleberry said. He walked toward Jaden. "That was one of the most intense — "

Hassleberry fell right into the river! He swam to the surface, coughing and sputtering.

Jaden ran to the river bank. "Huckleberry? You okay?"

Hassleberry grinned. "I owe you some Duel Disks."

Jaden smiled. "Oh yeah!" he said. "I was having such an awesome time I almost forgot. Thanks, admiral!"

Hassleberry started to correct him. "It's sarge — ah, never mind."

• CHAPTER FIFTEEN •

REPORTING FOR DUTY!

Later that day, Crowler and Bonaparte spied on the Slifer Red dorm. Chazz's workmen were busy working on his new room.

"It appears project 'Renovation Red' is almost complete," Crowler remarked. "This ought to drum up some publicity."

Bonaparte frowned. "This is all a *faux pas*," he complained. "We should demolish that dorm. Not let some rich slacker step in and give it an extreme makeover."

Then the men saw a boy marching toward the dorm. He carried a sack over his shoulder.

"Left . . . left . . . left, right, left," the boy chanted.

Crowler and Bonaparte looked at each other, puzzled.

The boy was Hassleberry, of course. He marched right up to the room shared by Jaden, Syrus, and temporarily, Chazz. He stomped into the room and dumped the sack on the floor. Books, dishes, and clothes tumbled out.

"Uh, Sarge?" Jaden asked. "Not to sound rude, but is there a reason you dumped your gear all over the floor?"

"'Cause I know you don't think you're bunking with us, right?" Syrus asked.

"Yeah," said Chazz, from his perch on the top bunk. "We don't need any freeloaders!"

Syrus glared at Chazz. "Yeah, you should know about freeloaders, Chazz." Chazz had parked himself in their room without asking, too.

"Yeah, well, what I meant to say was we don't need any *more* freeloaders," Chazz said.

"My mind's made up!" Hassleberry barked. "I'm giving

Troop Tyranno some time off. Anyway, Jaden showed me that I have a lot to learn."

"Oh no you don't!" Syrus said angrily. "Jaden's already got a best friend!"

"Besides, if you want to learn, you should really be following *me* around," Chazz told him.

Nobody responded to that.

"Hello? Anyone home?" Chazz asked.

Hassleberry ignored him. He looked at Jaden. "Hassleberry, reporting for duty!" he said. "This is truly an honor, sir!"

Jaden wasn't sure what to make of Hassleberry. But he figured he might as well go with it.

"You can call me Jaden," he replied.

Hassleberry saluted. "Sir, yes, sir!"